STEAMPUNK CATS WITH HATS

Luka Poe is a talented independent illustrator of adult coloring books. With intricate designs and attention to detail, they provide a relaxing and therapeutic experience for colorists of all levels. Their unique style often draws inspiration from nature and cultural motifs.

All rights are reserved Luka Poe. 2023
No part of this publication may be reproduced, stored in a retrieval system or transmitted in any form or by any means, electronic, mechanical, photocopying, recording or otherwise, without prior permission.

Welcome to our coloring book! Coloring is a fun and relaxing activity that allows you to express your creativity and imagination. Whether you're an experienced artist or just starting out, anyone can enjoy the benefits of coloring.

Coloring can help reduce stress and anxiety, improve focus and concentration, and promote mindfulness and relaxation. It's also a great way to spend time with family and friends, and a wonderful opportunity to explore different colors and designs.

Inside this book, you'll find a variety of images to color, from intricate patterns to whimsical scenes. So grab your favorite coloring tools and let your imagination run wild! Remember, there's no right or wrong way to color - just have fun and enjoy the process.

What you need to get started:

Coloring tools:

Colored pencils: these are pencils with a colored core that can be sharpened for precise coloring. They come in a variety of colors and can be blended together for a smooth gradient effect.

Markers: these are pens that come in a variety of colors and have a bold, vibrant appearance. They are great for larger areas and can be used to create bright, bold effects.

Crayons: these are sticks of colored wax that can be used to color in large areas. They come in a variety of colors and are easy to blend together.

Gel pens: these are pens that use gel ink and come in a variety of colors. They can be used to create detailed and intricate designs.

Coloring methods:

Blending: this is the process of combining different colors to create a smooth gradient effect. It can be done with colored pencils, markers, or crayons by layering colors and blending them together with a blending tool or by rubbing them together with your finger.

Burnishing: this is the process of using a colored pencil to blend and smooth out the colors, creating a shiny and polished appearance. It is done by applying heavy pressure to the pencil and blending it with a blending tool or your finger.

Stippling: this is the process of creating texture and depth by using small dots or dashes of color. It can be done with markers, gel pens, or colored pencils.

Cross-hatching: this is the process of using overlapping lines to create shading and depth. It can be done with colored pencils, markers, or pens.

These are just a few of the many tools and methods that can be used for coloring. The most important thing is to experiment and find what works best for you.

Thank you for purchasing my coloring book! I hope it brings you joy and relaxation.

I would greatly appreciate your feedback on your experience with the book. Your comments will help me improve future editions and provide the best possible coloring experience for others.

Thank you again for your support!

www.ingramcontent.com/pod-product-compliance
Ingram Content Group UK Ltd.
Pitfield, Milton Keynes, MK11 3LW, UK
UKHW060214240426
12048UKWH00031BB/1721